WHERE DID ALL THE SOCKS GO?

Medina Merritt

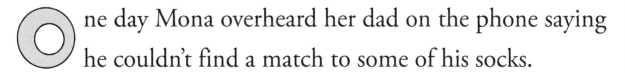ne day Mona overheard her dad on the phone saying he couldn't find a match to some of his socks.

Her dad said, "I only take them from the bedroom to the laundry room. I guess the machine ate it."

When Mona heard that, she became worried.

How did the machine eat it? she thought. *Is there a monster in there or something?*

On the car ride to school, she asked her father, "Why did you say the machine ate your socks?"

He replied with a smile, "It was only a joke, Mona. I didn't really mean the machine ate it. I just couldn't find them."

Mona thought about the machine monster all day. Mona got on the bus to head home and decided she would find out where her dad's missing socks really went.

It was dark, and the machine was running. Scared, Mona decided to walk in anyway. She tripped over something that was covering her leg, and she began to get nervous. She looked down and realized it was only a pair of pants.

She went closer to the machine, and it started to get louder.

Near the machine there were *thump thump* sounds.

She heard something moving but didn't know where it was coming from. Then she heard something breathing and started to scream.

"Mona, are you okay?" her dad asked.

He turned on the lights to find her pointing to the corner.

"No, Dad. I think I found the monster. The noise is coming from over there." She kept pointing to the corner.

He replied, "Where? That?"

He opened the door and turned on the light. It was only their cat, Sam.

Her dad laughed and said, "You mean this monster?"

Mona walked over and saw Sam. She turned to her right and saw a huge pile of socks.

"Dad," she exclaimed, "I found your missing socks!"

"Well, it looks like you did," he said, laughing.

Mona said, "It was Sam… I thought…it sounded like a…"
Her dad said, "Come look, there is no monster."

Mona said, "I guess the only monster is Sam."
They both laughed.

About the Author

Medina was born and raised in Long Island, New York. She is the third child out of eight children. Family has always been essential in her drive to make the world a better place for those who live in it. Her determination has since grown because of the birth of her beautiful young daughter. In 2017 she received her bachelor's degree in social work and is actively in the pursuit of securing her master's degree. She has always felt that education should be a priority but something that was fun. Through her experience with children, she found a great interest in making books that children could love to read. Medina wishes to tell a story through her work so that children can put their imagination into words. She feels that imagination and expression are both important in the development of children and hopes to reach as many children that she can through her work.

CPSIA information can be obtained
at www.ICGtesting.com
Printed in the USA
BVHW051552080721
611459BV00018B/1433

9 781662 423963